Home for Christmas

HOME FOR CHRISTMAS
A BANTAM BOOK 978 0 857 51360 1

First published in Great Britain by Bantam,
an imprint of Random House Children's Publishers UK
A Random House Group Company

This edition published 2013

Bantam Books are published by Random House Children's Publishers UK,
61–63 Uxbridge Road, London W5 5SA

www.randomhousechildrens.co.uk
www.randomhouse.co.uk

Addresses for companies within The Random House Group Limited can be found at:
www.randomhouse.co.uk/offices.htm

THE RANDOM HOUSE GROUP Limited Reg. No. 954009

A CIP catalogue record for this book is available from the British Library.

Printed in China

Home for Christmas

by Tish Rabe
based on a television script by Karen Moonah
illustrated by Tom Brannon

BANTAM BOOKS

One Christmas Eve
not long ago,
when everyone's yard
was covered in snow,
the Cat threw a party –
a Christmas event.
Everyone was invited
and everyone went.

There were jingle-bell cookies
and cranberry punch
and a gingerbread house
that the mice liked to munch.
Ralph won the Find-the-Most-
Candy-Canes game.
"Great party!" said a sea star.
"I'm so glad I came!"

Meanwhile, the Fish

looked at his Christmas list.

"Let's see . . . ," he said.

"Are there gifts that I missed?"

I'd like some fin lotion –
"Secrets of the Sea" –
and a pink plastic castle,
the right size for me.
And, Santa, please, if it's
not too much trouble,
a green deep-sea diver
who pops out of a bubble.
And now I have only
one more Christmas wish –
some Fin-Tastic fish food.
Thanks, Santa.
            Love,
               the Fish

When the Cat's party ended,
his friends waved goodbye.
Then he flew them all home.
(That Cat's such a nice guy.)
But when he took off for
Ralph's home in the snow,
there was a loud noise
and the Cat said, "Oh no!"

They heard a loud cranking.

They heard a loud creaking.

"Cat," Sally said, "I think

something is leaking!"

The Cat tried to steer,

but he knew in a flash

if he didn't land soon,

they were going to crash!

They landed somewhere
that was dusty and dry.
Then a family of elephants
came walking by –
an elephant mom
with her son and her daughter.

"Can you help us?" the Cat asked.

"We need to find water."

"Of course," said the elephants.

"That's what we do.

We can smell water

and we can help you."

So they took off again,
but the next thing they knew,
they crashed into the sea
in Blue-Puddle-a-Roo!

But as it turned out,

they did not get too wet.

They were saved by some dolphins

the Cat had just met.

Would they get home in time?

Would they miss Christmas Day?

"Push the Faster-ma-blaster,"

the Cat said, "right away!

To get home for Christmas,

it looks like we need

to fly through the air

at a much faster speed."

But something went wrong,
and the Cat had to land
next to some crabs
marching out on the sand.
"The Jiggermawhizzer
will not let me steer.
I don't think we'll get home
for Christmas this year."

It really looked like
everybody was stuck.
Had the Cat in the Hat
finally run out of luck?

But if you think the story
ends here, well, you're wrong.
The Cat in the Hat's never
out of luck long!

"Wait!" said the Cat.

"It's almost Christmas Day.

I'll give you your present.

Open it right away!"

"A present?" said Sally.

"Oh, Cat, that's so nice."

"Open a present?" said Nick.

"You don't have to ask twice!"

When they opened their present,
they got a surprise –
a small Thinga-ma-jigger
exactly their size.
"It's perfect!" said Sally.
"Let's fly it!" said Nick.

"To the Thinga-ma-jigger,"
the Cat said, "go quick!
I need you to tell me
what's broken inside."
"I'll drive!" said Sally.
And Nick said, "Let's ride!"

27

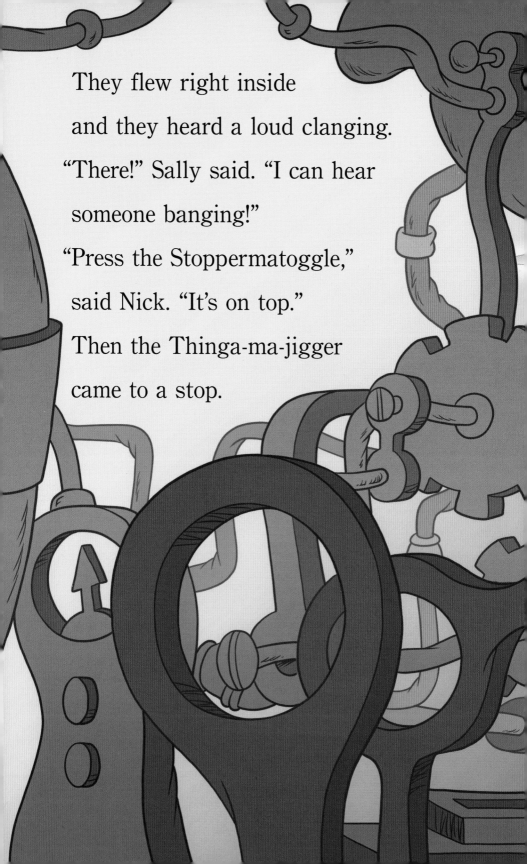

They flew right inside
and they heard a loud clanging.
"There!" Sally said. "I can hear
someone banging!"
"Press the Stoppermatoggle,"
said Nick. "It's on top."
Then the Thinga-ma-jigger
came to a stop.

"Please help me!" a mouse said.

"I made a mistake.

I only came in for

a little fruitcake.

My name is Fifi
and I can't get out."
"We'll help you," said Nick,
and he started to shout.

"Cat – there's a mouse in here!

What do we do now?"

"You save her," the Cat said,

"and I'll tell you how.

You need to hurry up

and throw the blue switch."

"But there are two," Nick said.

"Which switch is which?"

"Be careful," the Cat called.

"Pull the one that is bigger.

It opens the top of

the Thinga-ma-jigger!"

34

"Okay!" yelled Nick.

"Fifi, hold on tight.

He said pull the big switch.

I hope the Cat's right."

Nick pulled the big switch
and things started to shake.
"That's IT!" said Fifi.
"I'm giving up cake!"
"Get ready!" shouted Sally.
"Hold on! Here she comes!"
Then Fifi popped out . . .

. . . in a shower of crumbs!
"Thank you," said Fifi,
"for saving me.
Now I can spend Christmas
with my family.

I'm giving up sweets,

but it's really too bad.

That was the best fruitcake

that I've ever had."

"Glad you liked it," the Cat said.

"I made it, you see,

from my great-great-great-

grandma Cat's recipe.

I use special fruit.

Here, I'll give you a jar.

They're delicious, but I don't know

what kind they are."

So things all worked out,

as most stories do.

Ralph got home for Christmas

and Fifi did, too.

The Cat flew them home

and slowed down on the way

while the Fish dropped his

Christmas list in Santa's sleigh.

"Home for Christmas," the Cat said,

"is the best place to be."

"But something's wrong," Sally said,

"with the lights on our tree."

"Not to worry," the Cat said.

"I'll take care of that."

And he turned the lights on with . . .

. . . a flip of his hat!